Book #2

SECRET AGENT MJJ
The Secret Portrait

Marc John Jefferies

Big Smile Inc.

New York • Philadelphia • Los Angeles

Book #2

SECRET AGENT MJJ
The Secret Portrait

Marc John Jefferies

Written by: Danny Hirsch and S.A. Katz
Cover Illustration by: Doina Paraschiv

Produced by:
Marc A. Jefferies, Big Smile, Inc.

ISBN # 0-9761891-1-9
LCCN # 2005902277

The Secret Portrait
Written by: Danny Hirsch and S.A. Katz
Cover Illustration & Book Design: Doina Paraschiv

Printed in the U.S.A.
First printing March 2005

CONTENTS

A Letter To My Readers

A LETTER TO MY READERS

Dear Friends,

Thanks for picking up The Secret Portrait, the second book in the Secret Agent MJJ Series. I hope that you like it. To make certain that you enjoy it the best that you can, I've provided a Director's Sheet to help explain words that may be unfamiliar to you and a Gyroscope that explains some of the real people and places in the story. Both of these can be found in the back of this book and as always, if you need more information, check out a dictionary or your local library. Who knows? Maybe there you'll stumble onto your own adventures. Until then, read, enjoy, be kind to others and hang on tight because this ride is about to begin.

As Always,
-MJJ, The Real Deal

What you are about to read may surprise you. It still surprises me even after all that I have been through.

My name is Marc John Jefferies. Many of you may have seen me on TV or in a few movies. I am an actor and at thirteen I would say a pretty good one, not because of the roles that I have portrayed but because of the secret that I guard everyday. It is a secret that not even my family knows about. It is a secret that keeps the world safe and I am here to share it with you. You all know who I am in public. Now I will tell you the whole story; a story about the other me: Marc John Jefferies, the secret agent known as Boogieman.

ACT 1:
BOREDOM

Rainy days were even worse when I was stuck in school. Everything was gloomy and the fluorescent lights of PS 132 didn't help any.

I sat there on a Tuesday in my classroom listening to Mrs. Cooper, my social studies teacher, talk about the American Revolution. I couldn't concentrate. While she droned on and on about George Washington I was busy thinking about ancient Egypt and a secret organization called the Order of the Cat.

Why? Because two months ago I found out that I was a member of that organization. The order had been founded almost 2,000 years ago by an Egyptian queen to protect and guard world peace and justice. Two months ago, I, Marc John Jefferies discovered my true identity as the secret agent known as Boogieman. Two months ago I went on my first mission, to find a missing princess and stop a war-all while shooting a movie in the South Pacific!

You see, I'm an actor. That's my cover. My movie

career takes me to where the danger is. Only a few others know this secret. Many of them are now my new friends.

There is Glen, the director and writer of many of the movies that I have made. He is also a member of the Order of the Cat and as a child, he too went on missions. Now his job involves keeping me informed and making certain that I am in the right place at the right time, just in case trouble calls.

There is also Scooter Brosnan, codename Prepschool. Scooter is a few years older than me but we are now best friends, fighting the forces of evil together side by side. And we're having fun doing it too, if I may say so myself.

Then there is Princess Telia. As cute as she is, she's the toughest princess that I've ever met. Actually, she's the only princess that I've ever met.

And finally, there is the man who can not be forgotten, that mysterious silhouette known by the name Millenia. Millenia is a secretive figure. I've never seen his face, only a shadowy outline of the man and I do not know where he hides. All I know of him is that he has a gravelly voice and leads the Order of the Cat. There are rumors that he is thousands of years old. I don't really know. For now though, I guess that is enough.

All of these things ran through my mind as the rain poured down outside of my classroom window.

"Who can tell me what year the Declaration of Independence was signed?" asked Mrs. Cooper. "Marc John Jefferies?"

My head snapped up and I stared at her with a blank expression.

"Well," she said. "Do you know the answer?"

"1776," I replied without thinking.

"That's right," she beamed at me with a warm smile. "That is absolutely correct!"

Of course it was. Social Studies was my favorite class. I knew all of the answers. History came naturally to me. But today I couldn't think about patriots or the British. My thoughts were in the deserts of Egypt. I raised my hand.

"Mrs. Cooper," I said.

"Yes, Marc," she replied.

"When do we study ancient Egypt?" I asked.

"Why, not until next year," she responded. "This year is for American history. Next year is world history. You'll just have to wait."

She continued to smile as I lowered my hand. I couldn't wait a whole year but it appeared that there was no other way. The bell suddenly rang and everyone around me sprang from their seats.

"Lunchtime," proclaimed Mrs. Cooper.

I stood with everyone else and plodded off to find mushy tater tots and tuna surprise in the cafeteria.

And that's how the rest of the day went. The minutes slowly ticked by. All that I wanted to do was start on my next movie. Dad said that Glen was furiously at work on the script and that it would be done any day now. But I was impatient. I needed some adventure.

This carried on until the end of the day. When the

final bell rang, I bolted from the school and left the bus in the dust running the ten blocks back to my house. Why not? The rain had stopped and I was full of energy. I even did my homework right away when I got home. Still, I was bored. I played some video games, watched a little TV and went to bed. At least the American League Playoffs would be starting soon. I could always count on some baseball to cheer me up.

The rest of the week was much the same: school-work and mushy food in the cafeteria. Saturday finally came and it was a huge relief. The Yankees were going against the Twins later that night, so all I needed to do was keep myself occupied for the afternoon. I threw on a pair of Cons and grabbed my ball; I thought I would shoot some hoops for a while. But when I got downstairs and opened the front door, the rain had picked back up. Shooting hoops outside was out of the question. A little sad, I flopped back down on the sofa and clicked on the TV. Just then my mom walked in.

"Marc," she said. "What do you have planned for the day?"

I turned to look at her with sad eyes and an even sadder story.

"This is pretty much it," I said glumly. "Why? Do you have any ideas?"

"Actually, I do," she responded. "Would you like to come with me for the day?"

"Where to?" I asked.

"It's a surprise," she said. "But I think that you'll

like it."

"I'm game," I responded.

I jumped off of the couch, grabbed my jacket and headed out the door with my mom. Whatever she had planned was sure to be better than rotting on the couch with nothing to do.

Act 2:
THE COINCIDENCE

Well, maybe I should have known better. After all, my mom is a school teacher. A fun school teacher. But sometimes her idea of fun doesn't always match mine. Today was one of those days. The problem was I didn't know it until it was too late.

We arrived at the Metropolitan Museum of Art just as it was opening. 'Great,' I thought. 'The only thing quieter than our house on a Saturday afternoon is the Metropolitan Museum of Art.'

"Well," said Mom. "Here we are."

"Excellent," I said to her with as much enthusiasm as I could manage. She smiled at me and I decided it didn't matter where we were going as long as we could just hang out together.

We climbed the long stairs in front of the museum and skipped the line. My mom had a special pass that got her and a guest immediate admission. We wound our way through the halls past numerous paintings and sculptures by many people that I had never heard of. Every so often a name would jump out at me: Da Vinci, Van Gogh and Pollock. But I soon zoned out. This just wasn't my thing. Then my mother stopped walking.

"Here we are," she said.

I snapped to attention and looked at the room in front me.

"What is this section?" I asked.

"It's the Egyptian Art exhibit," she responded.

I looked up at her frantically. Did she know? Was my mother a member of the Order of the Cat? Was she in on the secret? Did she find out and if so how would I explain to Millenia that I had let the cat out of the bag? Hey, that's kind of funny.

"Mrs. Cooper called the house," Mom said.

"Whatever she said I didn't do it," I told her.

Mom laughed.

"Well, what she said was that you were asking about ancient Egypt in class the other day," Mom explained. "She told me that you were pretty excited about it."

"Oh, that," I replied. "Yes. That I did do."

My mom laughed again as I breathed a sigh of relief. My secret agent nerves of steel weren't quite ready for this kind of tension. Jumping from a helicopter at high speed was one thing. Having my cover blown by my mom was quite another.

I looked around the room. It was filled with hundreds of pieces of pottery and woven tapestry. Cases lined the walls with sparkling displays of gold jewelry and decorations. Broken pieces of stone with paintings on them hung alongside of these artifacts. I began to wander the room, staring in awe at these treasures. An hour quickly passed before I realized that I was definitely no longer bored.

"Marc," interrupted my mother. "There's still more to the exhibit."

She led me into another room. It was colder than the rest of the museum and darker. No sooner were we inside than a strange sight caught my eye. In the middle of the dimly lit chamber was a large stone box. I walked towards it. On the cover was the carving of what appeared to be a man but he was only my height. My mom joined me and read from the plaque mounted next to the display.

"This ancient sarcophagus was found in a small vault just outside of the city of Alexandria, Egypt," she read. "The mummy inside..."

"Mummy!" I exclaimed. "There's a mummy in there?"

"That's what it says," my mom replied. She continued to read. "Scientists have only been able to translate some of the carvings you see here. One of those translations is of a saying on the side that reads may victory smile. Unfortunately the rest of the saying has been damaged over time and scientists are unable to decipher the last pieces."

'May victory smile upon you!' I thought. The Order of the Cat! I quickly began to scan the box for what I knew must be carved somewhere on the outside. And then I saw it. Down by the feet of the carving was a small circle. In that circle appeared a cat's claws and cattails; those reedy plants that grow along the Nile. This carving was just like a pin that Glen had given me. It was the same as the pin worn by Scooter and probably Millenia. This carving was the sign of the Order of the Cat. I wondered who was inside.

Just then the lights went out. Excited murmurs could be heard in the dark.

"What's going on?" I asked.

A voice came out of the darkness.

"Alright folks," said a man. "Nothing to worry about. Just a power outage. Do not panic."

The voice was familiar and when I heard it a chill ran down my spine.

"Please follow the lit signs to the nearest exit," continued the man.

A flashlight gleamed in the corner as one of the security guards attempted to usher people out of the room. My mother and I turned toward the exit. We walked across the room and prepared to leave. The room was emptying slowly and my mom paused for a moment to speak with the security guard at the door.

"Sir, will we be able to come back into the museum today?" she asked.

I could not see the man's face. However, his badge caught some of the darting flashlight beams. In the dark it looked like a prism shooting tiny lasers around the room.

"I don't know, ma'am," said the man. "Please exit and wait outside for more details."

I knew that voice! But whose was it!? Just then the flashlight from the other security guard crossed the man's forehead. Still I could not catch sight of his face. But a familiar hint of green glistened from his eyes. I was just about to ask the man if we knew each other when my mom quickly pushed me out of the room and into the hallway.

"Sorry, Marc," she said to me. "If we can't get back in, we'll go somewhere else."

"Don't worry about it," I said. "But can we come back another day if they close the museum?"

My mom thought for a moment and then spoke.

"Of course," she said. "Tell you what. Let's grab some lunch and come back later. If we can get in, well, great. If not, then it's a date for next Saturday."

"You got it," I said. "But we can't stay out too long. Tonight is..."

Mom laughed.

"I know," she said. "The start of The American League Championship Series. Don't worry. I'll have you home in time to catch the first pitch on TV. I'd hate to have you miss that."

"Thanks," I said.

And we left to find some chow. My mind raced. It was amazing! I knew all about the Order of the Cat. Millenia had told me about it. But seeing the ancient Egyptian mummy and seeing the Order's symbol, the same symbol that was on my pin, Scooter's pin and on Glen's was just unbelievable. I couldn't wait to speak with Millenia again.

Act 3:
WE INTERRUPT THIS PROGRAM...

Mom and I ate lunch at a nearby restaurant and went back to the Metropolitan Museum of Art. Unfortunately though, it was closed for the rest of the day because of the power outage. We went home and once again boredom hit me smack in the face. I found myself right back where I started. The rain continued to pour outside and I was stuck inside.

"Oh, well," I said to the empty living room. "It's just you and me again."

I grabbed the remote from the TV, flopped back down on the couch and began to surf. Every channel was news. Great. That's just what I needed. Finally, I found a channel showing a rerun of the 2002 World Series. Excellent! This would be the perfect warm-up for tonight's game. It would definitely do!

It was the bottom of the eighth inning and I knew what was coming next. My dad had taken me to this game. Teddy Pluck was stepping up to the plate, the bases were loaded and I knew that the next swing

11

would be a grand slam.

But where was Henry James!? Even though it was a rerun, Teddy Pluck couldn't hit his homerun unless I was with Henry James! But he was in my bedroom. How could I get up the steps and retrieve my good luck charm without missing the play?

Just then, I remembered the Converse sneakers on my feet. These were no ordinary sneakers. Glen had given them to me for my first mission. The shoes had ultrajump technology and if I used the technology correctly, I could cover the distance to my room in three leaps.

I jumped off of the couch, stood up on my tip toes like Glen had shown me and jumped. I covered the 15 feet between the couch and the steps in one leap. I stood on my tip toes again and jumped another 20 feet up the stairs. Repeating the move, I leapt down the hall and landed safely and softly in my room. There on my bed was Henry James.

Who was Henry James you ask? Henry James was a stuffed bear of course. But not just any old Teddy bear. He was different. He was a Build A Bear that my mother had given me on my sixth birthday. I loved that bear and when my father took me to my first baseball game that year, Henry James (that's the bear's name), went along. Ever since then, the Yankees have not had a losing season. I refused to watch baseball without Henry James and the rerun of a game was not an exception.

I snatched Henry from the bed, repeated my three leaps and within seconds I was back in the living room.

I sat up on the couch ready for the big smash. The pitcher wound up and threw. Just as Teddy began to swing, the picture cut-out and a newsman appeared on the screen.

"We interrupt this program to bring you a special news bulletin," said the announcer.

Oh man. I just couldn't win today.

"Just moments ago a rare painting was reported stolen from the New York Metropolitan Museum of Art," said the newscaster. "Museum officials said that the culprits pulled off a miraculous heist. The painting was there when the room was inspected earlier in the day but after a morning power outage, a security guard reported it missing. It seemed to just vanish. The police are on the scene but as of yet there are no leads in the case."

That explains the blackout. My mind began to race. I wondered who had done it.

"More at eleven," said the announcer. "Stay tuned to channel..."

The Loop in my pocket rang. The Loop was a tiny device that looked like a cell phone. But it was more than that. It contained a GPS unit that could find me anywhere in the world. It also had a panic button on the back. If I hit that button, within five minutes a helicopter would appear to retrieve me no matter where I was.

I turned my attention away from the TV. The Loop rang a second time before I reached into my pocket and pulled it out. I was no longer listening to the announcer. On the third ring I flipped open the phone and answered.

"Hello," I said into the receiver.

A man answered on the other end.

"Marc John Jefferies?" he asked in an old, gravelly voice.

"Yes," I replied. "This is Marc John Jefferies."

"The world needs you," replied the man.

"Millenia," I said. "Is that you?"

"Yes Marc" he responded. "You must report to Glen immediately for a briefing. There is work to be done."

"Does this have to do with the stolen painting?" I asked. "I just saw it on the news."

Millenia chuckled on the other end of the line.

"Clever boy," he said. "Always one step ahead of the game. Yes Marc, it does. Now, Agent Boogieman, you must hurry. Time is of the essence."

With that there was a click on the other end of the line and Millenia was gone. So much for boredom. I quickly stuffed the phone into my pocket just as my mom reentered the living room.

"Marc," she said. "I know that it's raining outside but surely we can find something better for you to do than lay around on that couch all day. Maybe we could go to another..."

"You're right," I agreed.

"I am," said Mom with surprise. "Why, yes I am. Why don't you go out for awhile. Besides, we'll all be leaving town soon to shoot your next movie."

"Good idea, Mom" I replied smiling. "But I'm

already on it."

I jumped off of the couch, grabbed my jacket and an umbrella from the hall closet and headed out the door to find Glen.

Duty called.

Act 4:
THE LOFT

Glen didn't live far from my place but since it was
raining I decided to take the subway. I bought a ticket
from the machine, pushed my way through the gate
and jumped on a waiting train. It was packed with
people! It seemed that everyone else had the same
idea as I did. Oh well, at least I was dry. I kept the
hood on my jacket up so that no one would recognize
me. I love talking to fans but unfortunately time was
short today. Rather than run the risk of being rude
and unfriendly, I just tried not to be seen.

Within minutes the train pulled into Glen's stop.
The crowds pushed out and people poured onto the
platform. The waves of commuters and tourists
spilled through the gates and flooded the stairs with
both New Yorkers and other people from around the
world. The mass pushed their way up the steps
toward the street and the pouring rain.

I threw up my umbrella but the wind sent giant
drops flying under it. They pelted into me and

soaked the bottoms of my jeans. I ran the remaining block to Glen's and jumped under the overhang out in front of his building. A keypad was fastened to the wall by the door. I scanned the list for his name, jammed my finger into the button that was his and waited. The speaker crackled and Glen's voice came through. As always, he sounded a little frazzled.

"Hello," he squeaked. "Hellloooo."

"Glen," I responded. "It's Marc."

"Oh," he said startled. "Yes, that's right. I knew that you were coming. I did. Let me buzz you in."

The buzzer went off. The door clicked. I quickly grabbed the handle and let myself into the lobby where it was warm and dry.

Glen's building was old. It was once a vacuum cleaner factory and many of the old pipes and windows were still there. They had all been painted a bright color that made the building look and feel a little more like a home. Well maybe not like a home. More like some sort of carnival funhouse. Of course it looked like a funhouse, Glen lived there! Everything about it was sturdy looking though, including the iron elevator that sat at the opposite end of the lobby. I walked across the multi-colored tile floors, trying not to look down at the swirling and dizzying patterns. There was a huge red button on the wall and I assumed that it was for the elevator but I was sort of scared to push it. In Glen's building I'm always afraid that something is going to collapse or explode.

I gathered my courage and pressed the giant red button. The elevator groaned as it dropped toward its

17

lobby stop. The doors creaked open and I entered cautiously. I hit the button for the tenth floor and closed my eyes, hoping for the best. The elevator groaned again as it lifted me up and when I reached my stop, the contraption banged into place with a loud CLANG!

I slid the gate open, hopped out and knocked on the door in front of me.

"Who is it?" a muffled, anxious Glen called from the other side.

"It's Marc," I said.

"Marc who?" asked Glen.

"Marc John Jefferies," I said. "Glen, just open the door!"

The door opened a crack and two eyes peered out at me.

"So it is," said Glen.

The door closed once more. First I heard the rattle of chains and then the clacking of the door knob being turned. After of few seconds of banging and clanging, the giant metal door swung open with a huge BANG! There stood Glen. As always he was wearing a baseball cap. It sat on top of his tiny head. That tiny head rested on top of his skinny neck and narrow body. He looked just as he always looked when he was working on a movie: nervous and exhausted.

"Come in," Glen whispered. "And hurry!"

Same old Glen: he was all over the place. I stepped in and closed the door behind me. The apartment was just as I remembered it: a giant room with

30 foot tall ceilings and too many lights. I mean a whole mess of them. There were big lights, spotlights, small bulbs, lamps, nightlights and of course the giant chandelier.

In the middle of the room there was a single lonely desk. The only other furnishings were chairs. Chairs of all shapes and sizes were pushed against the walls on all four sides of the room. Dining room chairs, overstuffed chairs, bean bag chairs, bar stools and folding chairs all stood one right next to the other keeping watch on the center of the room where Glen's little workspace lived.

In one corner of the room there was a giant bowl of avocados on top of a short refrigerator. The bowl had a very elaborate design and looked expensive. The set-up reminded me of Glen's trailer on the movie set. Oddly though, unlike his movie trailer, this place was fairly clean-that is if you could ignore the giant pyramid of Spam tins stacked in the middle of an empty floor space by the kitchen sink. Likewise, a garbage can next to the desk was piled high with the pits and skins from eaten avocados.

"Glen," I said. "How many days have you been in your apartment working?"

Glen had already made his way across the room to the pyramid. He took a stray, empty Spam tin in his hand, climbed a short step ladder next to the pyramid and with careful movements placed the can atop the stack.

"How many weeks is a better question, Marc John Jefferies," Glen responded. "I have vowed not to leave

19

this room until the movie script has been written. I promised your father that and I promised him that I will not call until it is done. Tell me, if you were a sea turtle where would you swim to?"

He grabbed the brim of his baseball cap and shook it from side to side before looking back down toward me.

"Marc John Jefferies, I will find out where that turtle swims to and finish this script or, or, or..." he stammered. The lines in his forehead suddenly grew deeper and his voice became squeakier. "Or else."

"Or else what?" I asked.

"Or else or else," he said. "I don't know. That's the problem. Oh, these scripts! Why can't they just write themselves?"

"Millenia sent me," I said.

Glen let go of his hat and began to climb down.

"Millenia," he said. He looked around the room. The lines smoothed, he stood up straight and he suddenly became calm. "Yes, Millenia did mention that you'd be coming. But I already knew that...right?"

I nodded yes and then Glen nodded yes. He walked across the room to the wall opposite the door. He pulled a stool about three feet away from the wall and then reached toward his hat. After carefully gripping the brim, he removed his baseball cap. Out from underneath fell piles and piles of wavy blond hair. The golden locks fell in one movement down over his face until the entire mess suddenly collapsed onto his shoulders. I couldn't help but wonder if his hair had ever been cut.

20

When the last of it had finally fallen over his face, I saw a small, familiar looking satellite dish sticking out of the top of his head. He reached up toward it, plucked the item from where it sat and set it on the stool next to me.

"The POKEY," I said confidently.

"That's right," said Glen. "A petit operational kit with an electronic yap. A POKEY."

The tiny satellite dish was attached to a small grey box. A little keyboard stuck out from the side. This was the contraption known as a POKEY. Glen pushed a button and the device began to bark.

"I do love the electronic yap," he said smiling. "Now on to business."

And just like that the anxious, skinny Glen became a serious and businesslike secret agent. He suddenly pushed another button on the POKEY and a tiny lens popped out of its top.

"Lights!" shouted Glen. He clapped his hands twice...

CLAP! CLAP!

...and we were in darkness.

Suddenly the POKEY projected a blue light onto the wall right in front of us. The silhouette of a man's head moved into the picture. The shadowy figure began to speak.

"Greetings crime fighters," said the shadow. "What took you so long?"

Act 5:
THE MISSION

I stared at the familiar figure projected onto the wall.

"Hello, Millenia," I said.

"Boogieman," said the shadow. "Good to see you again. Are you ready?"

"For what?" I asked. "Am I going after the painting?"

"What painting?" asked Glen.

"There was a painting stolen today from the New York Metropolitan Museum of Art," I replied.

"Yes," said Millenia. "You are in search of the painting. First though, we must investigate and find out who has stolen it. Here is a photo of the missing work."

The screen flashed and Millenia disappeared. In his place the photograph of the painting appeared. It was a plain scene of a fence row and some pasture. A barn sat in the background and a tree stood on one side.

"It is a painting called *Fields* by Jaco Mifflin," continued Millenia.

It was something that my little sister would have liked but it just didn't look like it would be that expensive. Of all the famous paintings by all of the world's most famous artists sitting in that museum this one seemed like the least likely target for theft. Glen echoed my thoughts but said it all out loud.

"It doesn't look like anything famous. And I've never even heard of Jaco Mifflin," Glen said.

The picture flashed away and Millenia's figure returned. He was silent for a moment. He did not answer Glen's comment. Instead, he began to speak softly about other things.

"Boogieman," Millenia said. "You must go to Yankee Stadium. There you will meet Ron Gatling..."

"Ron Gatling!" I exclaimed. He was my all time favorite baseball player. "You mean Ron Gatling and the famous Gatling Blast!?"

"The one and only," said Millenia.

"Man," I said. "Ron Gatling. Will Scooter be joining me on this one? He'll definitely want to meet Ron."

"He can't," said Glen. "Scooter's on another mission in Central America."

"Darn," I said. "Oh well. I'll just have to get an autograph for him."

"Ron will help you gain entrance to the museum," said Millenia. "There you will have to photograph the area and look for clues. Before you go, Glen will give you the necessary equipment. Do you have any questions?"

"Just one," I said. "Who's in the sarcophagus at the museum?"

"What sarcophagus?" asked Glen.

"At the Metropolitan Museum of Art," I said. "I was there this morning and I saw a sarcophagus in the Ancient Egypt display. On the foot of the thing was the mark of the Order of the Cat. And he had may victory smile written on the side."

"You were at the museum this morning?" asked Glen.

"Yes," I replied.

"Did you see anything out of the ordinary?" asked Millenia.

"I was there during the power outage," I informed them. "The TV report said that the police believe the robbery happened during that time but other than the lights going out I saw nothing."

"It seems that our young friend is one step ahead of us, Glen," said Millenia. "Anything else?"

I remembered the voice that I thought I recognized and the green eyes. Neither thing seemed important. It was probably someone that I had met once while shooting a movie. Maybe it was a fan. I told Millenia and Glen just to be safe.

"But you have no idea whose voice it was?" questioned Glen.

"No," I said. "Maybe it will come to me later. Probably just a fan or someone that I once met during a shoot."

"Then good luck Marc John Jefferies," said

Millenia. "And may victory smile..."

"Wait," I said. "The sarcophagus. Who is inside?"

Millenia laughed.

"Most likely an old friend," he said. "Don't forget, our Order was started in Egypt almost two thousand years ago."

"But do you know who it is?" I inquired.

"Did you look on the label?" asked Millenia.

"The lights went out before I could," I informed him. "I know that there's a mummy inside but I can't believe that he's a member of the Order of the Cat."

"Can you believe that you are?" asked Millenia.

Good point.

"Not really," I said.

Millenia laughed.

"Then that mystery will have to be solved when you go back to the museum," he said. "But try to avoid taking care of it tonight. Sneaking in will be tricky enough. Now, as I was saying. May victory smile upon you."

With that the light disappeared and Millenia's silhouette was gone. Glen clapped his hands twice.

CLAP! CLAP!

The lights came back on.

Glen put one finger to his lower lip while he thought. He began to tap his lip slowly.

"Let's see," Glen said looking around the room as if to find something that he had lost. "Ah hah!" he exclaimed.

Glen ran across the room to the wastebasket sitting by the desk.

"Flip, flip," he called.

The basket spun around and spiraled into the floor. Not a single avocado skin or pit spilled as it did its little dance. No sooner did the basket spin itself into the floor than did a steel safe spin up and appear in its place. Glen bent down, twisted the dial on the front a couple of times and popped open the door. He reached inside and grabbed an item that I could not see. He closed the safe door and stepped back.

"Flip, flip," he said again. The safe spun into the floor and the wastebasket reappeared, the skins and pits still piled high inside of it.

"Marc, do you still have the Loop that I gave you?" asked Glen.

I reached into my pocket and pulled it out.

"You mean this one," I said.

"Yes," said Glen. "Let me have it."

I handed it to him and he took it.

"Millenia said that you'd need a camera to photo-graph the crime scene."

Glen handed me a Loop that looked exactly like mine. On closer inspection though, I could see a tiny opening on its cover.

"This is the updated Loop system," said Glen. "It has a built in micro camera that will let you take per-fect photos, even in the dark. The focus is instant. Just point and shoot."

Glen reached up toward the unruly pile of hair and scratched his head.

"Ah hah," he said again.

He raced back across the room and grabbed what

appeared to be the oldest chair in his collection. He turned it upside down and holding two of the legs in his two hands, said the password.

"Flip, flip."

Suddenly one of the legs spun and fell off of the chair. A small hole in the chair's seat became visible and Glen reached his fingers in. With his fingers he pulled a watch from the tiny space. He carefully set it on the ground, retrieved the leg that had spun off, held it to the space and said the words again.

"Flip, flip."

The leg spun into place and the chair was once again just as it had been before: old but usable.

"Put this on," he told me holding out the watch.

"Not again," I complained. "We haven't even been shooting a movie so I couldn't possibly have been late."

Once when we were shooting a movie on a remote island in the South Pacific, my mom gave me a watch. It wasn't a gift. Instead, it was a subtle hint that I was late for dinner one too many times.

"I know," said Glen. "But this little Swatch does more than tell time. You'll see."

I put the Swatch on and buckled it in place. It was a very cool looking piece. The watch had a silver face with a black band. Yes sir, it did look good on my wrist. It seemed to glow slightly. Glen lifted his hands over his head and...

CLAP! CLAP!

The lights went out. I couldn't see a thing.

"Marc," said Glen's voice from out of the darkness. "Can you feel the little button on the side of the watch?"

My hand ran over the face of the timepiece and to the side. The button was there just as Glen had said.

"Yes," I said.

"Push it," said Glen. "And please look away when you do so," he continued.

Glen was insistent and I did what I was asked. I happily turned my head away and pushed the tiny button on the side of my new Swatch. It was unbelievable. The entire room was lit up from the light beam that exploded from my wrist. Out of the corner of my eye I thought I saw Glen smiling. He looked pretty pleased with his latest secret agent device.

"What is this?" I marveled.

"We call it the Torch," said Glen. "There is a dial on the face of the watch. If you turn it to the left it will shine so brightly that the light can be seen from space. Turn it to the right and the light will tighten up to just a few feet."

I turned the dial to the right and just as he promised, the light condensed to just a few feet. Glen disappeared in the darkness.

CLAP! CLAP!

The overhead lights came back on. I immediately pushed the button on my new Swatch Torch and its light shut off. This time I could see the tiniest hint of green glow from behind the face. The second hand moved in steady ticks past each of the numbers.

"So," I said. "When do I meet Ron Gatling?" My excitement was getting the best of me.

"Tonight," said Glen. "I'll set it up."

"What do I tell my parents?" I asked.

"Just tell them that you're going to the game," replied Glen.

"The game," I said. "But it's the first game of the American League Championship Series. That game's sold out. No one can get tickets."

"Oh yeah," said Glen smiling.

He reached into his shirt pocket and pulled out a little yellow pass. I ran over to him and grabbed it. I quickly read the words printed on the front of the ticket. It was real! It was a pass to the game! I was going to the Yankees game!

"Admit One VIP To Any Ron Gatling Game At Any Time." I looked up from the ticket. "How did you get this?"

"I was Ron's roommate in college," said Glen. "We were best friends. Oh, and yes-he's a member of the Order of the Cat."

I gasped.

"Really! Cool," I said.

"You go and enjoy the game," said Glen. "I'll let him know that you're coming. Just make certain that you are waiting by the players' entrance one hour after the game is over."

"Got it," I assured him. "Ron Gatling and the Gatling Blast. I can't believe it. Aren't you coming with me?"

"I can't," said Glen. "I've got a script to write. I promised the studio and your Dad that I'd get it done ASAP."

Glen looked back over at his desk. His brow immediately furrowed and he began to fidget. I pocketed the ticket and walked toward the door as Glen began to talk to himself.

"Now," he said. "If I were a sea turtle where would I swim to?"

Poor Glen: stuck working and unable to go to the game. I opened the door to his apartment, walked out and closed it behind me. Just then, Glen came rushing out behind me smiling.

"If I were a sea turtle I'd swim to South Dakota," he said.

"Glen," I began. "South Dakota's not on the ocean."

"It's not?" he said.

"No," I told him. "It's surrounded on all sides by land."

"Well," began Glen. "The sea turtle could swim up the Mississippi and then go through the Missouri River..."

"Forget it, Glen," I said. "It's not on the ocean. You said a sea turtle; not a river turtle."

He gave me a sour look, turned around and went back into his apartment, slamming the door behind him.

"Just trying to help!" I called after him.

A moment later I heard a muffled voice from behind his door shout...

"Thank you!"

"You're welcome!" I shouted back smiling.

And I left for home to get ready for the game.

30

Act 6:
THE HERO, THE LEGEND AND THE MAN

I had been watching Ron Gatling play for as long as I could remember. Two years ago my father had managed to get us last minute tickets to see Ron in the World Series. But this year it was much harder and these were just the playoffs. Not a ticket could be found anywhere and here I was holding one VIP pass to see him play in the American League Championship Series! I only wished that I could have taken my entire family but I couldn't. It would be too hard to disappear after the game with them along. But there was someone who could come along with me: none other than the bear named Henry James. I crammed him into my backpack and headed out for the stadium.

I arrived at the park at about seven. I showed the man at the gate the pass that Glen had given me and within moments another man came to escort me to a VIP skybox seat. He opened the door and let me in.

"Help yourself to whatever you'd like sir," said the

man.

I looked around the room. Leather couches sat in the center. There were four different TV's to watch the game (or whatever else if your team was getting clobbered.) Next to one of the TV screens was a long counter with all kinds of sodas, juices and snacks set out. And they were good snacks. Real junk food, the kind of stuff Mom would not exactly be happy about me eating. But she wasn't here and I was pretty sure that Henry James wouldn't tell her. Now this was the way to watch baseball. I turned back to the man at the door.

"Thank you," was all that I could manage to say, my eyes bulging out as I made my way toward a bag of chips.

The man nodded his head, gently closed the door behind him and left me alone. Tightly clutching a bag of BBQ chips, I walked over to a large glass window that was the length of the room. Down below me were thousands of screaming Yankees fans. It was amazing! The air in the stadium was electric! The lights went down but the noise got louder. The walls thumped with the sound of the massive loud speakers booming the announcer's voice.

"YOUR NEW YORK YANKEES!!!!

Just then the lights flashed back to life and the place went completely insane.

I grabbed the handle on the window and slid it open. The roar of the crowd was deafening! The Yankees ran onto the field; all but one. The music stopped and the place got quiet. No one said a word because it was obvious what was coming next. Smoke filled the area in front of the dugout and then the lights went down again. The walls started shaking and I could feel the echo in my chest.

THUMP! THUMP! THUMP! THUMP...in a steady rhythm. The crowd screamed. There were two large flashes by the dugout and then the announcer...

"THE ONE. THE ONLY," he shouted over the loudspeaker. "ROOONNNN GAATLLIIING!!!"

The lights suddenly came back. It was magic. I thought that I'd seen it all in the movies but this was crazy! The smoke cleared, the speakers pounded and the crowd went bonkers. Ron Gatling was standing square on home plate. I looked around. All of the fans in the stadium were doing the Gatling Pump, just like Ron does before he hits a homer with the famous Gatling Blast. I'll admit it - I was in the box doing the double pump. My arm went up and down over and over as the crown screamed for Ron. This was perfect.

And so was the game. It was a nine inning pitcher's duel. A few hits but no score. It was the bottom of the ninth inning and Ron Gatling was coming to the plate.

He stepped into the batter's box. Every set of eyes in Yankee Stadium was fixed on him. With his left foot he stepped backwards out of the box and raised his hand for a time out. The pitcher stepped off of the mound. Ron took another step backwards and raised his arm again into the air, but this time he was gesturing toward the crowd. In two simple motions he brought every fan to their feet. It was a simple double pump but everyone knew what it meant. Ron was going to blast one out of the park!

"THE GAT-LING BLAST! THE GAT-LING BLAST!"

I joined in.

"THE GAT-LING BLAST! THE GAT-LING BLAST!"

Ron stepped back toward the plate, pointed his bat at the centerfield wall just like Babe Ruth used to do, put the bat back on his shoulder and waited.

The wind up. The pitch. Ron swung...

CRACK!

The ball took off like a rocket, sailing over the pitcher, the second baseman and finally the center-fielder before it carried over the 405 feet mark at the wall.

"THE YANKEES WIN!" shouted the announcer. "THE YANKEES WIN!"

I went nuts! I'd been standing for nearly two hours, my body half hanging out of the big sliding windows, not wanting to miss a single pitch. By the time the game was over I was completely exhausted. I grabbed a juice from the counter, plopped down on one of the couches and looked at my watch. An awesome box seat, the Gatling Blast, a Yankees win-and I still hadn't even met Ron yet. In one hour, this would definitely go down as one of my greatest nights ever.

Act 7:
THE STADIUM

I anxiously stared at my watch waiting for the time to tick away. The lights were already out in the stadium and I could see people hard at work cleaning the stands for tomorrow night's game. Finally the hour passed. I jumped up and headed out the door in search of the players' entrance.

I ran back the way I had come and once in the parking lot, followed the signs to a small door away from the regular entrances and parking area. There were no lingering fans. Everyone had already left the parking lots. The people had come and gone with the players whose autographs they were after. The place was abandoned. A dim light shone over the entrance and as I approached I could make out the silhouette of a security guard.

"Sorry kid," he said. "All the players have gone home already. No more autographs."

Just then the door opened.

"He's with me," said a man in a Yankees jacket.

Ron Gatling!

"Sorry, Mr. Gatling," said the guard. "I didn't know that you were still here. Well, goodnight then."

"It's okay Sal," said Ron as the guard walked away. "Have a good night." Ron turned to me. "You must be Marc," said Ron extending his hand for a shake.

I shook his hand.

"Pleased to meet you, Mr. Gatling," I stammered. I was in awe.

"Call me Ron," he said smiling. "Agent Boogieman." He winked. "Oh, before I forget..."

He handed me a rolled up poster.

"This is for Scooter, Agent Prepschool," said Ron. "Glen said that you'd be asking for it."

"Thanks," I said still in shock as I stuffed the poster into my backpack.

Ron motioned for me to follow and we went through the player's entrance and into the belly of the stadium. The hallways were quiet as we navigated the maze. We stopped at a door marked LOCKER ROOM. Ron took a key card from his jacket, slid it through the scanner and opened the door.

The long hallway had been dark and it took a few moments for my eyes to adjust to the bright overhead lights of this new place. When I could finally see, my jaw dropped. The Yankees locker room! All of the greats had gotten ready for the game here. Mantle, DiMaggio and oh yeah, Babe Ruth. I was stunned and could do nothing but stare. The Pharaohs of ancient Egypt may have had the pyramids but Yankee Stadium was nothing less than the eighth wonder of the world for any true baseball fan.

"Come on," said Ron smiling. "We've got work to do. You can gawk later."

Ron walked over to a door on the other side of the room marked FIELD ENTRANCE.

"This way," he instructed. "You can leave your backpack here. It'll be safe."

"I'll just take it along," I said.

"Why?" asked Ron. "It'll just slow you down."

"Don't worry about it," I told him. "I'll be fine."

"Does it have special equipment of some sort inside?" asked Ron.

"You could say that," I said.

Ron looked at me suspiciously.

"What kind of equipment?" he asked.

I realized that Ron was not going to let this one go.

"Ron, I'm about to tell you something that can't leave this room."

"Shoot," said Ron.

I slung the backpack off of shoulder, pulled out Henry James and told Ron the entire story. Ron smiled.

"Is that it," he responded. "Why don't you go over to Teddy Pluck's locker and look inside."

"But Ron," I protested.

"Don't worry about it," he assured me. "Teddy won't mind."

I walked over to Teddy's locker and looked inside. There it was, the twin of Henry James. Teddy Pluck kept a Build A Bear in the clubhouse! I turned back to Ron but when I did, I couldn't believe my eyes. The great Ron Gatling was standing there in the middle of the New York Yankees locker room holding a Build A Bear just like mine. I was just a little confused.

"Everyone's got one for good luck," said Ron smiling. "Well, everyone except for Bobby Schiller."

"What does Bobby keep for good luck?" I asked.

"A moldy blueberry muffin," said Ron. "Turns out his wife baked one for him before our first win and he refused to throw it away until the season ended."

I went to Bobby Schiller's locker and there it was: a moldy blueberry muffin. Nasty. Baseball players were more superstitious than I thought. I looked around at the other lockers and sure enough several players had there own Build A Bear.

"You're right," I said.

"How else can you explain our winning streak? Just leave the backpack and the bear here," said Ron. "I'd hate for us to lose the playoffs because Henry James was misplaced."

I set my bag and bear carefully on Ron's chair. Then I followed him out the door and down the long hallway towards the field. We came to a door marked "PLAYERS ONLY." Ron turned the knob and walked through.

"Follow me," he said.

I took two steps down and found myself standing smack in the middle of the dugout. I was actually standing in the Yankees' dugout! How cool!

"No time to hang out, Marc. We'll stop back here another time. Follow me," he insisted.

I couldn't help it. Ron was already on the field waiting for me but I needed another second to take it all in. Thirteen years of watching Yankees baseball. I couldn't help but sit on the bench for a moment. I did and it was just like I was part of the team. I was in a daze when I heard Ron's voice.

"Now hitting for the New York Yankees, number ninety nine, Marc John Jefferies!," cried Ron.

I looked up and saw Ron standing on the top step of the dugout smiling down at me.

"You know that your mouth is wide open," he said with a chuckle.

"Sorry," I replied closing it.

"Don't worry about it," said Ron. "So was mine the first time I hit the field. Tell you what. Why don't you take a quick trot around the bases."

I didn't hesitate. Instead, I stepped up to home plate. I held an imaginary bat in my hands, waited for my imaginary pitch and hit a walloping imaginary grand slam out of the park. Then I took a victory lap around the bases. The stands were empty and the place was dark but I could hear the fans shouting my name.

'Marc! Marc! Marc!'

Ron was waiting for me by home plate with his hand up for a high five. I tapped the plate with my foot. Ron and I slapped hands.

"Nice hit, agent Boogieman," said Ron. "Just like the pros."

"Thanks," I said standing next to the famous player. "Now where do we go?"

"We're here," he said. "Flip, flip."

And we were suddenly in the dark.

Act 8:
DOWN UNDER

Ron and I stood side by side in a small dark room. "Where are we?" I asked.

"Under home plate," said Ron. "You don't know how many times I've wanted to say 'flip, flip' when Ralphy Rodriguez steps up to bat. That man can hit the long ball."

"Why did you hide the entrance under home plate?" I inquired. "Won't someone find it here?"

"The best place to hide anything is right under someone's nose," explained Ron. "Millenia taught me that. Besides, would you have looked for an entrance here?"

"Entrance to what?"

"Flip, flip," Ron said again and we spun around into another dark hallway.

I couldn't see anything.

"Did you bring some light?" asked Ron.

I felt around on my watch for the button. I pressed it. The room lit-up with a green glow.

40

"Wow," he said. "Where did you get that?"

"It's one of Glen's little toys," I replied.

"It's amazing" he said stepping forward. "I always trip when I'm looking for the switch."

Ron reached out and flipped a switch on the wall. The room lit-up revealing another door at the opposite end. A boy sat in a chair next to it.

"Could you turn down the Torch, mate?" said the boy. He had an Australian accent. "My eyes have just begun to adjust to the dark. It's rather nice, truly."

"The light on your wrist," said Ron. "Turn it off."

I switched it off as quickly as I could.

"Thanks," said the boy. "It's a little hard to see with all that glow, you know."

The boy stood. He was my height with long straight black hair and big brown eyes. He smiled a big toothy grin. He was dressed from head to toe in khaki and had on knee high boots.

"Agent Boogieman," said Ron. "Meet Jim Tawley, AKA: Agent MoleRat."

"Gooday'," said MoleRat. "Or should I say goodevenin'."

"Jim flew in today to help us with this assignment. He's going to take us to where we need to be," said Ron.

"To the museum?" I asked.

"That's right," said Jim.

"But the museum's closed at this time of night," I said.

Jim smiled a toothy grin.

"Not for us." He threw his hand over his shoulder

motioning for us to follow. "Step this way."

He opened the door on his end of the room and walked through.

"Where are we going?" I asked Ron.

"Underground," said Jim.

"Where, on the subway?" I asked.

Ron smiled.

"Sort of," Ron said.

I shook my head.

"You'll see," said Ron.

We went in after Jim.

"Okay, if you please," said Jim. "Your light mate."

I pressed the button on the Torch and lit the space. A long narrow staircase descended to the bottom of a giant tunnel. Twisted train tracks ran along the floor and disappeared into the darkness.

"Where are we?" I asked.

"Old number 71," explained Jim. "This'll take us where we need to be. Come on then."

We walked down the steps, my light bouncing off of the walls. We reached the bottom of the steps and turned left. The floor was littered with small stones and a few rocks the size of someone's head. I had to be careful so I didn't trip.

"Is this tunnel still used for anything?"

"No," said Ron. "It's been abandoned for decades. Jim discovered the tunnel not too long ago, shortly after another of our secret corridors filled with water.

"That's right," said Jim. "I built a tunnel so long and perfect that you could walk just about anywhere in Manhattan. That's why they call me the MoleRat because I'm a real tunnel tiger. But with all of the rain, the one that used to lead to the art museum is temporarily closed. So here we are."

"Why would we need a tunnel to the museum to begin with?" I asked.

"We've got tunnels everywhere," said Ron. "New York's a great city but you and I both know that something's always happening. The tunnels are just in case. We could go anywhere in this town. Well, just about anywhere. New Jersey's still a bit out of reach."

We walked along the tracks until we came to some water. The ground disappeared into the murky pond.

"Now what," I said.

"Not a problem mate," Jim said. "Turn your light to the right."

Along the water's edge was a small rowboat.

"Hop in," said Ron.

Jim and I jumped in and Ron pushed us into the water. At the last second he climbed aboard. I felt a little uneasy. My last adventure aboard a boat was almost a disaster. I just hoped that this time I wouldn't have to abandon ship. Ron grabbed the oars and began to row. We skimmed across the water at good speed.

"It's actually good luck for us that the other tunnel did fill-up all the way," said Jim. "It's a mighty walk. Five miles to the museum. I'd much rather float there than hike."

We continued on into the abyss, my green Torch flickering off of the dripping damp walls.

We passed an old train car flooded with the water. Its windows were broken out. The wooden sides were rotting and it made the spooky surroundings even more frightening. Shadows from my light danced off of the water and through the rail car making it look as if there were a group of ghosts frolicking inside.

"Nifty trick, those shadows," said Jim.

"Yes," I responded as a chill ran up my spine. "Nifty. Real nifty."

The tunnel turned a corner and the cavern opened up.

"This was the old East River Harlem Crossover," said Ron. "My dad helped to dig this station but it was never used. Most people don't even know that these tunnels are still here."

"No one else can get in here, right?" I asked.

"Absolutely not," assured Ron. "The Order of the Cat sealed all of the entrances after we found the place just so people wouldn't wander in and get lost. This is no place to play."

"My idea," beamed Jim. "Didn't want to have to come down here and retrieve anyone, even though I do love a good crawl space."

Jim flashed his toothy grin again.

We passed through the station and entered into another long shaft. More rail cars littered the stream. Just then, out of the darkness rose a hideous sight. Ron and I jumped.

"What is that?" questioned Ron with alarm.

A long claw cast a shadow on the ceiling of the

tunnel and moved as we came closer. It was three times the size of our boat, and it looked sharp.

"Turn up that light, mate," said Jim.

I turned the dial and the place lit-up brighter than a beach on a summer's day. This Torch was amazing!

"Just what I thought," said Jim. "An old steam shovel."

There it stood, rising out of the water like a sea monster. Its iron shovel hung off of a long steel arm. The cab was partially sunken under the water.

"She's beautiful," said Jim. "Too bad she's just left down here to rust."

"Yes," said Ron with uncertainty in his voice. "Too bad."

Ron continued to row on. Soon we caught sight of the end of another abandoned car.

"Turn down the light, Boogieman," said Jim. "We're getting close."

Our boat bumped into the back of the old train car. Jim jumped up, grabbed the door, opened it and stepped in.

"Toss me that rope, Marc," said Jim.

I grabbed a coiled rope that was sitting in the bottom of the boat and threw the end to Jim. He quickly tied it to the side of the car.

"Come on," said Jim running into the car.

I looked up and aimed the Torch at the train car. It was buried in stone. Just the back end stuck out. I turned to Ron.

"Is this a good idea?" I asked him. "I mean, he knows what he's doing, right?"

45

"I don't know," said Ron. "This is my first time working with him."

I sighed.

"May victory smile upon us," I said.

I jumped from the boat and into the car. Ron followed.

"Bring your light this way," said Jim.

The inside of the car still had all of its original furnishings. The old benches were still there, although the highly polished wood was cracking and covered in slimy green and purple mold. Cobwebs hung everywhere but the spiders had long since given up and left. The musty smell was overwhelming for a moment. The far end had collapsed from the weight of the stone above but in the middle of the rubble was a small door about three feet wide and three feet tall. Jim reached out and pulled it open.

"After you mates," he said.

I ducked my way in. Ron had to crawl through on his hands and knees. Once again we were in total darkness. I clicked on the Torch and the cramped crawl space was filled with the eerie green afterglow.

"You two crawl about twenty feet that way," said Jim closing the door behind him. "At the end of the tunnel, you'll come to a dead end. Call the password and you'll spin into a storage closet on the ground floor of the museum. From there you can use the Loop to navigate your way through the ventilation shafts."

"What about you?" I asked. "What are you going to do?"

Jim pressed his ear to the wall of the tunnel.

"I'm gonna' stay here and make certain that the tunnel stays up while you're gone," he said smiling.

"Do you think that it's going to collapse?" asked Ron.

"Naw," said Jim smiling. "But you can never be too safe. Besides, there's no sense for all three of us to head into the museum. I'll wait here for you. Good luck."

Ron and I crawled slowly into the darkness and just as Jim had promised, we came to a dead end.

"Flip, flip," I whispered.

The wall swung around and suddenly I found myself sitting in a storage room in the New York Metropolitan Museum of Art, in the dark, in the middle of the night with baseball legend Ron Gatling. Could my life get any stranger?

Oh yes, it could. Read on.

Act 9:
RETURN TO THE SCENE OF THE CRIME

Ron Gatling and I sat in the dark of the supply closet in the New York Metropolitan Museum of Art. "Now what?" Ron whispered.

I looked around the room. The soft glow from the turned down Torch lit our surroundings. I glanced around the room and realized that we were in the janitor's closet. The shelves were lined with all sorts of cleaning supplies and there was a small ventilation hatch in the ceiling. I tapped Ron on the shoulder and pointed up to the tiny opening. It was just big enough for me to fit through

"If I can get into the vent system, I can avoid the security guards."

Ron looked at me, "You're going to have to go alone. I couldn't possibly fit in there."

I took a deep breath and sighed.

"Let's do it then," I said.

Ron gave me a boost up. I climbed off of his lift and onto the top of one of the storage shelves. The vent cover was attached by two small screws.

"Ron," I said. "I need a screw driver. Do you see anything down there that I can use?"

Ron looked around. He lifted a few things off of the shelves.

"I can't find anything," he said.

I thought for a moment and then said, "Wait a minute. Do you have your car keys?"

He reached into his pocket and pulled out a small ring.

"Yes," he whispered.

"Hand them to me," I whispered back.

Ron tossed the keys in the air and I caught them. I took a key and put the edge of it into one of the slots. Carefully I turned the key in the screw. The screw began to turn with the key. It worked!

"Anything?" whispered Ron.

"It's working," I whispered back. "Almost there..."

Soon the first screw fell out of the hole. I quickly went to work on the second. Before I had a chance to brace the vent cover, the whole thing fell from the ceiling and landed on Ron's head.

CLUNK!

"Ron," I whispered. "Are you okay?"

"Fine," he said.

He took off his hat and there, perched on top of his head, was a POKEY. The satellite dish on it was clearly bent.

"I don't know about the POKEY though," said Ron.

"Are you okay?" I asked again.

"Don't worry about me," he called. "Do you have the Loop?"

"Yes," I said. "Glen gave me the updated model with the camera installed."

"Perfect," said Ron. "Use the Loop's tracking system to make your way through the vents. When you get to the gallery room where the painting was, check for clues and then report back here at once. I'm going to try and find a junction box in this closet somewhere. If I can hack into the museum's security system, I might be able to download the security camera tapes from the day of the theft."

"You got it," I said. "Good luck."

"You too," said Ron.

"Do you have enough light?" I asked.

"Yes," said Ron. "I think that there's a light somewhere on the POKEY."

He pressed a button and the device began to bark. He fumbled for a moment with the controls before finally shutting it off. We both froze, waiting to be caught, but no one came.

"Electronic yap," said Ron. "I'll never forgive Glen for that one."

I smiled and shimmied my way into the darkness of the vent. Once inside I fished the Loop out of my pocket. I turned it on and a map of the ventilation system flashed on the screen showing my location and the location of the room that I was looking for. I crawled forward slowly on my belly, inching along by the glow of the Torch, being careful not to make a sound.

I passed over an open grate. Down below I could see marble statues. Rows of faces stared up at me as if they knew I was in the vent. The museum was definitely more exciting by night. Something moved!

'It must be my imagination,' I thought. Then it moved again! I froze. A shadow crept across the floor and I watched from my ceiling perch.

Click. Click. Click. Click echoed the steady sound of footsteps just before a security guard passed beneath me. I breathed a sigh of relief and continued to move forward slowly.

I came to a dead end. I looked down at the Loop. This couldn't be right? I pressed the reload button. The map disappeared and a moment later reappeared. Still, it showed that I should be able to go through. I looked again ahead of me and sure enough, the vent was blocked. I didn't know what to do. And then I heard the humming.

First the hum was soft and then it got louder and louder. I could feel air start to move by me. My shirt tale began to blow as the speed of the wind picked up. I tried to back up but the wind was too strong. Suddenly, the blockage ahead of me swung open with a loud...

CLANG!

The air shaft opened with the sudden burst of fresh air through the system.

I quickly crawled forward and just as I passed the swinging piece of metal, it crashed closed behind me.

CLANG!

The wind stopped and once again everything was

quiet. I sighed in relief and moved ahead toward the room.

I turned a corner and my path was stopped once more by a grate. I turned the dial on the torch and the space lit up. There were no screws to remove. I pushed against it with my hands. It did not move.

'Well,' I thought. 'There's only one other thing to do.'

I turned my body around in the cramped space and put my feet against the grate.

"May victory smile upon me," I whispered before giving the cover a swift kick.

The cover flew off and a moment later I heard the racket.

CLANGETY, CLANG, CLANG, CLANG!

I waited and when I heard nothing, I pressed a button on the Loop. Ron answered the call on the other end.

"Hello," crackled his voice.

"Ron," I said softly. "I'm at the room."

"Great," he replied. "I've scrambled the video security in the room. You should be able to move around in there without being spotted."

"Roger," I replied. "Boogieman out." I love saying that.

I slipped out of the space and into the room. I was at ceiling level and right below me was a giant statue. Carefully, I dangled my feet out of the vent hole in the ceiling and onto the statue's head, slithered down the side of it and landed on the floor of the room. I surveyed the scene.

The entrance to the place was marked-off with yellow police tape. An empty space on the wall showed where the painting should have been. I looked around the room some more. It still did not make any sense. The museum was filled with paintings by Picasso, DaVinci, and Monet, all famous artists that could bring a thief more money than the stolen painting.

I looked some more. Nothing. I took the Loop out of my pocket and photographed the area. As I was shooting the room the Loop began to vibrate. I put it to my ear.

"Hello," I whispered into the receiver.

"Boogieman," said Ron on the other end. His voice was crackling. "I've been able to tap into the security system. I can see someone coming your way. I think that..."

The signal faded. What a time for the POKEY to go out! Then I remembered the broken satellite top and understood why he was unable to finish what he was saying. I ran over to the statue and just as I was about to climb it, I saw something on the floor.

A small object caught my eye. I bent toward it and picked up a small piece of plastic the size of a credit card. It had a magnetic strip on one side and the words 'Fountain Inn Suites Hotel' on the other. It was a hotel room key; the kind that you swipe through the door. I put it in my pocket. It might be a clue.

Suddenly, a flashlight shined in my direction.

"Who's there?" said a security guard from behind the police tape.

Caught! I had to think fast. There was no way to climb the statue in time.

"Come here," he said.

Quick, what to do. I reached down, turned the dial on the Torch all the way to the left, turned around and pointed the light at the security guard's face.

"Ah!" he exclaimed dropping his flashlight after being stunned by the light. That was the opportunity I needed. There was no way that I could shimmy into the vent in time. I had no choice. I ran right at him and at the last second, dove onto my belly, sliding underneath the security tape and past the guard.

"Safe!" I exclaimed.

I jumped to my feet, turned the dial back to the right so that the Torch was dark and ran.

I looked down at the Loop. Turn left, turn left, turn right two halls down, turn right again turn left. Another flashlight bobbled ahead of me.

"Hey!" shouted a voice.

I covered my face with my hood to keep from being seen and charged right at him. I stopped dead in my tracks, stood on my tip toes and took off like a rocket over his head.

"What the . . . . How . . . Who," he cried as I flew over him.

"No worries buddy," I yelled as I hit the ground running. I looked back down at the Loop. Turn left, right bingo! The closet! I opened the door and hopped inside.

"Who's there?" called Ron.

"It's me," I said. "Did you download the security tapes?"

"Yes," replied Ron.

"Good," I replied breathlessly. "Then let's get out of here. The security guards will not be far behind!"

We quickly slithered into the hole in the wall. Ron went first.

"Flip, flip," I called, and the shelves slid back into place covering our escape. Jim's toothy grin greeted us in the tunnel.

"Gooday' mates," he beamed with his smile. "Did we get what we came for?"

"Let's hope so," I said. "Because I don't want to do this again. Now we've got to get out of here, fast!"

Ron chuckled as we made our way back to the boat and safety.

Act 10:
EVIDENCE

After our close call at the Museum we all made our way home safely. The next day I went over to Glen's to meet with Ron and Jim and look over what we had gathered. When I arrived Millenia's shape was already projected onto Glen's wall.

"Welcome," said Millenia as I entered the room. "Good job at the museum."

"Thank you," I replied. "Ron, did you get a chance to go over the security tapes from the day of the robbery?"

"Right here," responded Ron.

He pulled the POKEY from under his cap and showed the tapes on the wall next to Millenia's outline. It was the same room that I was in last night and the painting still hung on the wall. A hulking security guard came into the room, looked around and then pulled a walkie talkie from his belt.

"This is the weird part," said Ron.

The guard pressed a button on the walkie talkie

and a second later the screen went dark with the blackout. When the lights came back on, the painting was gone.

"Unusual," said Millenia.

"Can you adjust the picture so that we can see a face?" asked Glen.

"Negative," said Ron. "His head's down the entire time."

"Wait a minute," I said. "Rewind it. I think I saw something."

Ron rewound the tape so that we could watch it again.

"Pause it!" I yelled. "Look."

I ran up to the picture and pointed to the guard's hand.

"Look at the ring," I exclaimed.

It was a gold band with a purple stone in the center.

"Excellent eye, Boogieman," Millenia said. "It's a small lead but a clue nonetheless. Glen, run that through the computer and see what you come up with."

"You got it," responded Glen.

"What about your photos, Marc?" asked Ron.

"I examined them this morning," I replied. "There was nothing there."

I reached into my pocket and retrieved the hotel key.

"But I did find this last night," I said.

Glen took the key from me. Then he pressed a button on the POKEY and a small pad popped out of the side. He passed the key over the pad and suddenly, below Millenia's shape, appeared the address of the Fountain Inn Suites Hotel and the room number that the key belonged to.

"Fountain Inn Suites," said Jim. "That's a rather swank spot for a crook to gully up."

"What?" said Glen.

"I think you know where you need to go next," said Millenia. "May victory smile upon you all." And with that he disappeared.

"We've got time before the game, Marc," said Ron. "My car's outside. Let's go check out that hotel."

"You got it," I said.

Glen's face looked perplexed.

"Are you coming along," I asked him. He pointed to his computer and shook his head from side to side.

"I can't," he said. "I'm still trying to finish the script. Good luck."

Ron, Jim and I raced off to find the Fountain Inn Suites Hotel.

Act 11:
THE CULPRIT

The rain had stopped and the skies were refreshingly sunny. Midtown Manhattan was alive with the sounds of car horns. People filled every street corner and walked in and out of different stores.

The three of us arrived at the hotel, left the car with a valet and walked up to the entrance.

I'm an actor, and many people recognize me wherever I go. And Ron...the man's a superstar. People gawked at us as we walked on the sidewalk. They whispered to one another.

"Hey, isn't that Ron Gatling."

They waved and made the pump sign.

"Hey Ron! Way to go last night. The Gat-ling Blast! The Gat-ling Blast!"

Yes, that's right ladies and gentleman-I know Ron Gatling. Yes, we are friends. Yes, he's going to give me an autograph. I smiled broadly. What kid wouldn't?

"And Marc John Jefferies," said some others. "Hi Marc!"

I waived.

"What, are you two famous or something?" asked Jim with a puzzled look on his face.

Ron stared at him.

"A little," said Ron. "Don't you own a TV?"

"Naw," said Jim. "You saw the kinds of places I like to hang out in. Now tell me, where would I plug one in?"

This kid's a riot.

"Ron," I said. "Jim's got a point."

"What, that you can't plug a TV into the wall of a tunnel?"

"No," I said slowly. "We're too famous. We're going to draw a lot more attention together. Maybe we should split up."

"Good idea," replied Ron. "You two enter here. I'll go around back. When you walk in, just pretend like you own the place. But stay low."

"No worries," I assured him. "Come on Jim."

Ron raced off around the block with a crowd following. Jim and I ran into the hotel. We crossed the lobby and reached the elevator. I pressed the button for the fifty-second floor.

"We're looking for room five two five two," I reminded Jim.

The elevator took us up over fifty floors to our stop. We exited into an elaborate entryway. We snaked through the plushly carpeted hallways and past the elegant decor of the ritzy hotel and finally found our door.

"Room five two five two," said Jim.

Just then Ron appeared from the other direction. He was breathing heavily.

"What happened to you?" I asked.

"I ran up the stairs to escape the crowd," he said.

"Fifty flights?" said Jim.

"I'm an athlete," said Ron.

"Right," I replied.

Ron looked to his left and his right and after making certain that no one was around, he removed his baseball cap revealing the POKEY. He pulled it from the top of his head, typed something into the keyboard and then waited.

"What are you doing?" I asked.

"Scanning the room," Ron replied. "To see if there's anyone inside."

A moment later a green light began to blink on the side of the device.

"Coast is clear," said Ron as he once again removed his cap and hid the POKEY under it.

I pulled out the keycard, swiped it through the lock and waited. The red light on the knob turned to green and then I heard the CLICK that said that the door was unlocked. Ron turned the handle and led the way into the room.

It was a typical hotel room: two beds, a desk, a television and a dresser. We searched the closet and all of the drawers. Nothing. I decided to go through the trash but again, no clues surfaced.

"Seems that we've wasted our time," shrugged Ron.

"There must be something here," I exclaimed.

"Let's check one more time. Did anyone look under the bed?"

Suddenly I heard the familiar CLICK of the door lock. Someone was coming!

"Hide," I whispered.

Ron ran for the bathroom. He jumped into the bathtub and quietly pulled the shower curtain shut behind him. Jim and I dove for the bed and wiggled underneath it. I looked to my left and saw Jim smiling. I raised my eyebrows as if to ask him 'What's so funny?' He pointed down. Next to me was the surprise of surprises: the missing painting! Why didn't anyone look under the bed!?

I had no time to think about it because three people entered the room. From my vantage point I could only see the bottoms of their trousers and their shoes. But judging by the size of the feet on the three people, I knew that they were all very big.

"Where do you want us?" said a deep voiced man.

A fourth pair of feet, much smaller than the others, joined them in the room.

"Two of you men guard the door," said another man, his voice very familiar to me. "The other man will stay with me and watch the window. Go to it. I need to make a phone call."

I heard the door open and then close. The smallest pair of feet walked over to the other side of the bed. He must have sat down on it because the mattress slunk low putting pressure on Jim and me and making the small space even smaller. I could hear the phone being lifted from its receiver. Whoever was dialing seemed to be in a hurry because it sounded as if they were punching the keypad instead of just pressing it.

"Hello," said the familiar voiced man. "This is Foulton."

Dr. Foulton! That's the voice of Dr. Bartholomew Foulton. I knew that I recognized his slimy sound. And it was the same voice from the man at the museum! It was the same Dr. Foulton that I had faced in another case. I listened closely to his side of the conversation.

"Are we still on for 11:30 tonight?" said Foulton into the phone. There was a pause before he said, "No! Why not?"

He stopped speaking and tried to interrupt several times but was unable. He finally got a word in.

"Well then when!?" demanded Foulton. "Fine, I'll be there. What's the address?"

There was another moment of silence before Foulton again spoke.

"Hold on," he growled impatiently into the phone. "I've got a pen and paper right here. Let me write that down."

I could hear the scribbling of a pen on paper and then the tearing as Foulton ripped the sheet from the notepad.

"I'll see you then, and..."

Foulton suddenly stopped speaking as if he were interrupted.

"Yes, I have the painting," he said, his voice becoming louder.

Just then, a hand reached down between the two feet and began to grope around. Jim and I dodged the hand as it moved back and forth finally bumping into the painting. Foulton quickly latched on and pulled it from under the bed. So close!

"You'll get it Friday," Foulton said. "And then Millenia and the Order of the Cat will pay for all that they have done to us both."

I considered rushing out and trying to grab Foulton but then I remembered the big guy in the room. Besides, even if we overpowered the two of them we'd never be able to take on all four. I waited. Now was not the right time.

"Then it's settled," said Foulton. "Eleven thirty on Friday night. Goodbye."

And he slammed the phone down onto the receiver.

"Take the painting," ordered Foulton to the man.

I watched the second set of shoes in the room walk over to where Foulton was. A moment later, the bottom edge of the painting appeared by his feet.

"What's wrong?" asked the man.

"It seems that our buyer is very nervous," said Foulton. "He refuses to come to New York until some of the heat has died down from the robbery. We'll have to hide out for a few days until he arrives. And he wants me to come alone.

"Alone," said the man. "I don't think that's a good idea boss."

"I don't think that's a good idea boss," said Foulton in a mocking tone. "You don't get paid to think. Don't forget, I'm the boss around here. In the meantime, let's keep moving. It's not safe to stay in one place."

"Got it, boss," said the man.

"Let's go," said Foulton.

The mattress sprang up giving me more room. Then the four feet moved out of sight and with them the painting. I heard the door open and then close and the room was once again silent. I waited a moment before crawling out of my hiding space. I looked around the room one more time before speaking.

"Ron," I whispered. "I think that they're gone."

I heard the ring of the shower curtain sliding back and Ron suddenly appeared from the bathroom.

"Dr. Foulton's got the painting," I said.

Ron ran out the door and looked both ways.

"He's gone," said Ron. "Should we try to follow him?"

"That won't do any good," I said. "It's New York. Once they hit the sidewalk, they're gone. But Foulton did say something about an 11:30 meeting on Friday. It appears that Foulton is not working alone on this one. If we go to that meeting we can nab everyone involved. We need to be patient and wait."

"Agreed. But how do we find out where they're meeting?" asked Ron. "I heard the entire conversation and Foulton didn't say a thing about the place they were going."

I walked over to the notepad that sat on the night-stand by the bed. Foulton had indeed torn off the sheet that had the address written on it. But what he didn't take was the sheet underneath it.

"Quick, Ron," I urged. "I need a pencil. Do you have a pencil?"

"Yes," he responded. "Why?"

"Give it to me," I said. "I have an idea."

Ron reached into his pocket and pulled out his keys. Attached to the ring was a key chain that looked like a tiny bat. He turned the end of it and a small piece of lead came out of the end.

"Will this work?" asked Ron.

"Perfect," I exclaimed taking the pencil from him.

"I saw this once in an old movie," I explained.

Foulton had pressed down too hard and left a slight impression on the piece of paper underneath his note. This was our lucky break. I shaded lightly over the dents in the paper and as I did so, the light outline of an address appeared.

"I got it," I beamed. "It's Liberty State Park."

"Liberty State Park," said Jim. "Where's that?"

"On the other side of the Hudson River," I said. "It's in New Jersey but right on the harbor."

"You can take a ferry from the park to Ellis Island and the Statue of Liberty," explained Ron. "And there's an old abandoned train station there too. It's a very historic spot..."

The Loop in my pocket rang.

"Boogieman." It was Glen. "You know the ring that you spotted on the security tape? I ran it through the computer. It was purchased two weeks ago by a B.B. Foulton. It's Dr. Foulton that stole the painting!"

"We know," I replied. "He was just here."

"You know?" said Glen with a puzzled sound. "He was there? What?"

"I'll tell you all about it later," I said. "You know what's really odd?"

"What's that?" asked Glen.

"Foulton looked huge on the tape," I said.

"Probably just a big coat," said Glen. "You know a disguise or someplace to hide the painting."

"Yes, but..."

"Oh, no," said Glen. "Oh, not again."

"Glen, calm down," I assured him. "We know where he's going. We'll get Foulton."

"It's not Foulton that I'm saying oh no about," said Glen. "It's my computer. It crashed again. Glen out."

Glen hung up and a moment later the Loop ran again.

"Are you stopping back here to check-in?" Glen asked.

"Right away," I told him.

"Great," he responded. "Glen out."

Glen hung up a second time and I put the Loop in my pocket.

"What was that all about?" asked Jim.

"Writers," I said.

And we all left to go check-in with Millenia.

Act 12:
PLANNING

Glen, Jim, and I decided to discuss the case while we watched Ron play that evening's game. We met each other in the VIP box at the stadium just before the start of the game. Glen closed the shades on the big window and walked over to the entrance door to lock it. Within minutes we were staring at Millenia's shadow on the wall.

"Are we at a baseball game?" asked the secretive Millenia.

"Yes," said Glen sheepishly.

"Most excellent," said Millenia. "It's been a long time since I was at a game. Will you leave the POKEY on after we talk so that I can watch?"

We all looked at one another.

"Sure," I said. "If you'd like."

"I would," said Millenia with a gleeful chuckle. "Now, update me."

We told him about the hotel and Foulton and we explained how close we were to the painting but how it was too dangerous to move. And we told him about the meeting that would take place on Friday.

"Good thinking, Boogieman," said Millenia. "Always using your head. What next?"

"It's near a national landmark," I said. "It's going to be hard to get in and out of there."

"You leave the arrangements to me," said Jim. "First thing Monday morning I'm taking a little tour of the area to find a way in. Marc, you want to go with me?"

"I can't, Jim," I explained. "I've got school. Hey, why aren't you in school?"

Jim smiled his toothy grin.

"I'm from Australia, mate," said Jim. "Different time of year. I'm on Holiday you know."

"Holiday?" I asked.

"I think you'd call it vacation," said Jim.

"I think that I'd call it lucky," I said.

Everyone laughed.

"Then Thursday it is," said Millenia. "Now, I believe the game is starting."

We opened the shades and turned our attention to the field. Just then, I remembered Henry James. Oh no! He was still in Ron's locker downstairs from the other night's game! I couldn't watch a game without him. It was bad luck.

There was a knock at the door. I went over to answer it. I opened it and there stood a stadium employee.

"Mr. Jefferies," said the girl.

"Yes," I replied.

She held out my backpack to me.

"Mr. Gatling thought that you might need this," she said with a smile. "Oh, and he'd like for your party to come down to the locker room and meet the team after the game. He said that he owes you an autograph."

I took the bag, unzipped it and looked inside. Henry James stared back at me. I quickly closed the knapsack.

"Thanks!" I said closing the door behind me.

Jim turned around and saw me.

"What's in the bag, mate?" he asked.

"Victory," I explained with a smile.

And I sat down to watch the game. The Yankees soon took the field. Thankfully, I had my bear with me.

That night's game wasn't even close.

Act 13:
WAITING

Sunday night brought another fabulous Yankee win. After the game we visited Ron in the locker room. We met all of the players and I got all of their autographs. And Glen, believe it or not, actually relaxed and took a much needed break from writing his movie.

But then Monday came. Jim researched ways to get into Liberty State Park, Glen went back to his desk and Ron left for game three in Boston. I went to school and the endless boredom attacked me again. I was getting pretty good at this secret agent stuff and all that I wanted to do was save the world and go on to the next mission.

As I sat in class, my mind wandered to Liberty State Park. I wondered how Jim would get us in. Would we go from Manhattan across the water to Ellis Island and then the drop point? Or would MoleRat find a tunnel? I was daydreaming at my desk when Mrs. Cooper called my name.

"Marc John Jefferies," she said. "Do you know the

answer?"

"Ellis Island," I said. The class laughed and I blushed.

"Ellis Island," she said. "We're learning about the War of 1812 today. My goodness. First it was ancient Egypt and now Ellis Island. You've certainly gotten ahead of the class. The section on Ellis Island is at the end of the year."

"But I..." was all that I could say before Mrs. Cooper interrupted me.

"Tell you what," she said. "Since you're so excited about the subject, see me after class and I'll give you some more homework."

"But..."

"Good for you, Marc John Jefferies," she said with a smile. "It's nice to see that someone is excited about history in here."

Oh, man. I smiled at my teacher, sat up and paid attention, anxiously awaiting Friday.

After class, I took my extra homework and went home to do it. From there the week dragged on. Tuesday was much the same as Monday. Actually, Tuesday was worse than Monday. That night I watched the Yankees get pounded on television. Ron didn't even get a hit. And then Wednesday-oh, Wednesday! Again, the Yankees lost. It was worse than before. What was happening? Thursday was a day off from Baseball while the teams traveled back to New York. Thank goodness. I didn't know if I could stand to watch again. And then Friday finally came. Finally!

Action.

Act 14:
HENRY JAMES TO THE RESCUE

On Friday night, I sat once more in the VIP booth as my Yankees, the Bronx Bombers, waited to take the field. Jim was with me and we were both hoping for a victory.

"Did you find a way in?" I asked Jim.

"Sure did, mate," said Jim. "And it's a doozy."

Then the rain began to fall outside. The big infield tarp would be coming out soon. Grounds keepers rolled the giant cover over the grass just as the sky opened up. It began to pour. A moment later, the door burst open.

"Marc," said Ron. "There's a problem."

"What is it?" I asked.

"The game," said Ron. "It's been delayed on account of rain."

"How long?" asked Jim.

"How long will it rain," said Ron. "Who knows? You two might have to go to the meeting without me."

"No way," I said. "Don't worry. The game will start soon."

"If there even is a game," said Ron. "It's pouring. Besides, we haven't played very well the last two games. Hopefully it'll be over quickly. I can't take another loss like the last two."

"What happened to you guys out there?" I asked. "You-you were horrible."

"I know," said Ron. "The pitching is off and Teddy Pluck's not hitting. And Bobby Schiller lost his lucky muffin."

"You mean the moldy one," I said.

"That's it," replied Ron.

Jim looked at the two of us with an odd expression on his face.

"This muffin you're talking about," said Jim. "It wouldn't happen to have been a nasty looking little piece of baked good, would it have?"

"The nastiest looking muffin you have ever seen," I told him. "Why?"

Jim put his head down.

"Well, the other night when we went down to the locker room," began Jim.

"Yes..."

"Well, I do believe I ate that muffin," confessed Jim.

"What!?" Ron and I said at the same time.

"How was I supposed to know that it was some ballplayer's good luck charm," argued Jim. "And even though it looked all fuzzy it really was quite a tasty morsel."

"Oh, disgusting," I said.

"Man, what's Bobby going to say now," said Ron.

I thought about it for a moment. An idea crept into my head. I walked over to the door where my backpack sat. I picked it up and brought it over to the guys.

"Ron," I said. "Lend him this."

I unzipped the bag, reached in and pulled out Henry James. I handed the bear to Ron.

"But only for the series," I said.

"What about you?" asked Ron. "Don't you need him for the game?"

"Bobby needs him more," I said.

Jim looked at the stuffed bear.

"What's that mate?" he asked.

"Victory," Ron replied with a smile.

Ron took Henry James and left the VIP box. Moments later the sky cleared up and the game began.

The Yankees crushed their opponents in game five of the American League Championship Series. Ron played a perfect game and twice, to the chants of "THE GAT-LING BLAST! THE GAT-LING BLAST!" he hit homeruns, both nearly going out of the park. He was a man on a mission and that mission was to end this game as soon as possible. And he did just that, throwing out player after player, picking-off base stealers like Renaldo Martin from his place behind home plate and calling every pitch like a good catcher should to help the guys on the mound strike out as many as they could. The Yankees as a team soon drove up a score that would be impossible to come back from. By 10:30, the damage was done and the Yankees were now one win closer to the World Series. I pulled out the Loop and hit the panic button to call for a chopper. Before I could head downstairs to congratulate Ron, he reappeared in the VIP booth.

"Are you ready," he said as he entered.

"That was fast," I responded, a little shocked with his speed. "Great game," I shouted.

"Thanks," he replied. "And Bobby Schiller says thanks too."

"Henry James to the rescue," I responded. "But only until the end of the series."

"Right," said Ron. "Where's our ride?"

"Across the street," I told him. "There's an old fire escape up the side of the building that we can use. But how can we get past the crowd? After a win like that, everyone's going to be hanging around outside."

"Across the street," said Ron. "That's easy. The stadium and that office building are connected. We'll just run through the clubhouse. Forget the fire escape. Just head down the private steps toward the dugout entrance. We'll cut through the stadium tunnels."

"You got it," I replied.

Ron took over the lead as we ran down the steps and through the clubhouse. A couple of players were around and I high fived them as I ran by. Within minutes we were across the street. As we headed up the staircase toward the roof of the now empty office building, I could hear the roar of the helicopter engines. I swung the door open and the wind generated by the copter blades nearly knocked me off of my feet. Ron was right there to keep me up.

"Take us to this address, pilot!" I shouted over the engines.

"Roger, Agent Boogieman!" shouted the pilot in response.

And we took off into the night, headed for Liberty State Park.

Act 15:
AMBUSH

The helicopter sped through the night sky, swooping low over the ground and staying tight to the water's edge to keep from being picked-up on radar by anyone in the area. Soon we were nearing Liberty State Park. The massive New York skyline shimmered behind me and I began to wonder how I was ever able to get bored in such an awesome city.

We made our way over the water in search of our target. We turned hard to the right and the pilot informed us that we had arrived. An open field was beneath us with large gas tanks next to it. We flew a couple more blocks north.

"We're near, sir!" shouted the pilot. "I'll drop you a couple of blocks away, just so that we don't raise too much suspicion! Will I be landing or will you be jumping?!"

"Why, jumping of course!" I shouted with a smile.

"Jumping!" exclaimed Ron. "But I'm wearing cleats!"

I opened a small compartment under the seat, reached inside and pulled out a pair of shoes.

"Put these on!" I called back to him handing him a pair of Converse sneakers with ultrajump technology just like the ones that I was wearing.

"I'm always prepared," I said to him.

"What about Jim?" Ron asked.

Jim lifted his foot showing the bottom of his boot. There was the logo: CONVERSE.

Ron put on his shoes and when we got close to a low building in the area, all three of us stood up on tip toes.

"Ready!" I shouted. "Now!"

And we all jumped, landing at the same time, quietly and gently, on a tiny warehouse. Jim quickly located a fire escape and we all made our way to the ground. I pulled out the Loop, checked the directions and followed the GPS coordinates toward the park where the meeting would take place.

We quickly closed the distance to the park. Jim ran to a shadowed area by a fence that surrounded the parking area. We followed him along the edge to another building. In front of that building stood a mailbox. After making sure that no one was around, Jim stepped behind it. He peered around the corner.

"Coast is clear," said Jim.

"Is there a tunnel around here," asked Ron.

"Naw," said Jim. "Not quite that exciting. Follow me."

And he ran along the fence even further stopping at a particularly rusty section. He stopped and so did we. There, in the fence, was a large hole.

"Did you make that?" I asked.

"The rain did," said Jim. "See how rusty it is. Who's first?"

Ron darted through the hole. I was close on his heels. Jim followed. The three of us ran across the parking lot toward a building by the water's edge. The place was deserted but we stayed low just in case.

When we reached the building we stopped.

"Do you think that they're inside?" I asked.

"I don't know," whispered Ron.

"Doubtful," said Jim. "I've been watching all week and the park guys lock it up pretty tightly at night. Keep a lookout."

We slowly made our way around the perimeter of the building. Every shadow that moved looked like a bad guy. Every sound was someone waiting to spring on us.

We came upon the old train station. It was just as spooky as the tunnels. The platforms were still there but weeds had grown up around where the tracks once were.

"Immigrants used to take trains from here to places all over the United States," said Ron. "My grandfather was one of them."

"Wow," I said. "All of the people..."

I didn't finish what I was saying.

"Hello," said a man from the dark. It was Foulton! I was certain of it this time. Never again would I forget the harsh notes in his evil voice.

We all dove down on our bellies staying low beneath the weeds. I slowly lifted my head and peered out over the area. Had he spotted us? A skinny figure moved just a couple of platforms away. That had to be him.

"Hello," said Foulton again. I could see the rectangular outline of the painting in his hand.

"Don't come any closer," said a deep, booming voice from out of the darkness.

The silhouette of a large, hulking man appeared and stood opposite Foulton. Although my eyes were now adjusting to the light, I could not make out a face on the new man. Only his outline showed and for a moment, he reminded me of Millenia. He did not leave the cover of the shadow.

"Do you have the painting?" said the deep voiced shadowy figure.

"Right here," replied Foulton. "But first, show yourself so that I know that I'm giving this to the right person."

The shadow with the deep voice laughed a loud booming laugh.

"Does this prove my identity," said the man as he flung a small suitcase out onto the platform. "Open that and count it. Then you'll know that I am who I say I am."

Foulton carefully approached the suitcase and bent down toward it. He opened it with the hand that was not holding the painting and then reached inside. Pulling out a stack of one hundred dollar bills, he again looked toward the mysterious figure.

"Not good enough, Trufo," said Foulton.

"Trufo!" said Ron to me in a low voice. "He's the Leader of the Order of the Snake! I should have known."

I suddenly realized that I had the new Loop with the camera. I slowly held it up and snapped a picture of Foulton holding both the money and the painting.

The shadowed Trufo then flung a small canister out toward Foulton. The doctor dropped the money and caught the canister in mid-air.

"Spray that on the painting and then you'll have the proof that you need," said Trufo.

Foulton gathered the money and the canister and stepped back to a safer distance. He popped the cap off of the canister and used it to spray the painting from top to bottom, then left to right. The colors began to run and then bleed into one another and as they flowed down the front of the canvas making the scene disappear, a new picture began to show in its place. Foulton's eyes widened as the paint came off of the frame and covered his hands.

"Yes," he said. "This is it."

The pasture and the barn were gone and in their place was a portrait of an old man. I again pulled the new Loop from my pocket and took a picture of the secret portrait. Millenia would want to know about this. Foulton turned his attention to Trufo.

"I have what I came for," said the doctor. "I believe that this belongs to you."

And with that, he flung the painting across the platform. It landed squarely at the feet of Trufo.

"Now what?" Jim whispered to Ron and me. "He's destroyed it. We've failed."

"We were sent to retrieve that painting," Ron replied. "That painting. And that's what we're going to do. Remember the mission."

I thought about it for a moment and nodded my head.

"You're right," I responded. "We need to follow orders and get that painting back, no matter what it is. Or what he's done to it. Or whatever. We have a job to do so let's do it."

"Right on," said Ron. "I'll distract them. You slip in and grab the painting."

"What'll I do mates?" asked Jim.

"Stay here and back me up," said Ron.

Jim popped his head out of the cover and looked at the two figures.

"Two on two," said Jim. "Right. You got it. Piece of cake."

Ron removed both of his shoes.

"On my signal," Ron told me.

"Good doing business with you," said Foulton with a smile to Trufo. "And here's to the end of that dreaded Order of the Cat."

Ron looked at me and then jumped up.

"Now!" he shouted.

The two men turned to look at Ron. I darted out of our hiding space right for the painting.

"Who's there?!" said Foulton.

He reached out to grab me just as Ron yelled...

"Over here!"

Foulton looked up and as he did so, I slid on the ground just like I was stealing home and just like I did to the man in the museum. I glided between his legs. Ron hurled one of the shoes as if he was trying to throw out a man at second base and knocked Foulton off of his feet.

"You're out!" Ron yelled.

I dove and grabbed the painting at Trufo's feet.

"Mine!" yelled Trufo.

Ron hurled his other shoe but Trufo ducked at the last second, dodging the throw. I looked up to see Trufo still coming at me. Just as he reached me, a boot whizzed by my head and hit him squarely in the face. I turned to see Jim standing next to Ron smiling. Jim looked up at the world famous catcher.

"You said to back you up," said Jim.

"That I did," said Ron. "When you grow-up you might make a good relief pitcher."

"Thanks mate," said Jim. "But we've still got some work to do."

Jim turned to Foulton.

"The game's up, Foulton," announced Jim. He pulled his Loop from his pocket and hit the panic button on the back to alert the helicopter crew where we were at. Foulton rolled around on the ground for a moment. Clutching his head, he jumped to his feet.

"I got my money," said Dr. Foulton. "And the Order of the Cat will soon be finished. Wait till next time. You'll see."

And he turned to run.

"Not so fast," said Ron.

84

Ron jumped up on the platform and took off after Foulton. He quickly caught up to him and with a burst of energy, leapt forward and tackled Foulton. Ron pinned Foulton down just as Jim came running up.

"You thought you could outrun me," said Ron to Foulton. "Do you know how many bases I stole last year?"

"I didn't know that there was tackling in baseball, mate," said Jim. "Where'd you learn to do that?"

"In college I played football in the fall," said Ron. "Four years."

Meanwhile, I was still trying to solve my own problem. I turned to run away with the portrait but just as I did I was yanked back. Trufo had the other end of it!

"It's mine," he thundered. "Give it to me."

His hulking shadow loomed over me and although I could not see his face, I was afraid. I did not know how much longer I could hold on. An idea came into my head. I suddenly let go. Trufo stumbled backwards but did not fall.

"Mine," he declared.

"Not for long," I assured him.

I hit the button on the Torch and turned the dial all the way to the left, blinding the mysterious man.

"My eyes!" exclaimed Trufo as he covered his face.

I charged him again and grabbed the painting. I tugged as hard as I could but he would not let go. Just then, the whole thing gave way. The frame broke apart and the canvas, old and frail, split down the middle. I fell backward with half of the secret portrait in my hand.

"You!" shouted Trufo as Jim came running to my aid. "This is not the last you'll hear from me."

He grabbed his half of the painting and ran.

"He's getting away," said Jim.

I dropped my half of the painting and began to run after the shadowy figure. He darted across the parking lot. We gave chase. Our helicopter was just landing on the cement but Jim and I ran past it. Trufo did as well covering his face with his hands. He was approaching the front gates. I thought we had him cornered but just then a black Porsche came out of nowhere and drove right through the fence! It spun around and stopped. Its passenger door swung open and Trufo hopped in with the torn painting in hand. The car turned around and sped out of the area.

"To the helicopter!" I instructed.

Then I remembered Ron. I called out to him.

"Are you okay?!" I shouted.

"Go!" shouted Ron. "I've got it under control here!"

We ran to our ride and climbed aboard. Lifting off, we could see the Porsche driving on the roads below, turning corners at break-neck speed and narrowly missing other cars as it tried desperately to escape us.

"Pilot!" I shouted over the chopper's engine. "Don't lose that car!"

The Porsche quickly turned and suddenly went back the way it came.

"What's he doing?" asked Jim.

The car spun this way and that and was soon back in the parking area of Liberty State Park. But instead of slowing down it sped up.

"He's trapped!" said Jim.

We flew out ahead of him and landed on the dock between the car and the water. But just before the Porsche reached us, it skidded to a stop. We waited in the helicopter to see what would happen next. Suddenly, the wheels on the car spun, smoke rose from the pavement and the car turned sharply to the right. A small fin rose up out of the top of the vehicle and the back spoiler spun around to reveal two propellers. The car smashed through the barrier at the edge of the dock and crashed into the water! The propellers began to spin and after bobbing for a moment, water shot up into the air, the car turned over and disappeared under the water.

"After them!" I commanded.

Jim and I jumped from the helicopter. We reached the water's edge. I was the first to dive in with Jim following close behind. I hit the water smoothly and once under the surface, I turned the dial on my Torch to light the area. I looked to the bottom. There sat the Porsche. I tried to swim towards it but it was no use. The propellers spun faster and the car drove away—under water!

I swam back to the top, took a breath and looked around. Just then Jim appeared next to me.

"Did you see that, mate," said Jim. "That car drove right away. Underwater even."

"And he has half of the painting," I said. "We better report back to Millenia."

We climbed back up onto the dock and walked over to where Ron was still sitting on top of Foulton.

"What do we do with him?" I asked.

"Why send him to jail of course," said Ron.

I picked up our half of the secret portrait and we loaded ourselves and our captive into the helicopter. Ron continued to hold Foulton down. I dropped the ripped painting on the floor next to him. Some rescue. We had destroyed it. My half was part of the nose, mouth, and chin of the old man. His eyes and the top part of his face were missing.

Suddenly, I felt a pit in my stomach.

"It's ruined," I exclaimed.

Ron took the piece from me and held it in his hands. He then looked at me.

"We did our best," he said.

Foulton began to laugh.

"What's so funny?" asked Jim.

"Stupid brats," said Foulton. "You have no idea what you've got there, do you."

"We've got a secret portrait," I said. "A ruined secret portrait."

"Don't be so sure," chided Foulton. "Things aren't always as they seem. Stupid kids. You risked all of this and had no idea what you were after. Fools."

"What are you talking about?" said Jim. "We've destroyed the secret portrait. Does anybody know what he's talking about?"

"Ask Millenia," said Foulton. "But I'm sure he didn't tell you for a very good reason."

"You're lying," I said. "He's trying to confuse us with this."

Foulton laughed again.

"Have it your way," said Dr. Foulton.

"Pilot," said Ron. "Take us back to Glen Spade's apartment." Ron looked to Foulton. "On the way, make certain that you stop at police headquarters. We have a delivery to make."

"You can deliver me to any police you like," said Foulton. "But without the original painting they won't have a case."

"Maybe they won't have the painting," said Ron. "But I'm sure if they test what's on your hands they'll have more than enough paint."

I looked down at Foulton's hands. They were still covered in the paint that had run off of the secret portrait. Then, I carefully removed the broken canvas from the frame.

"Would this help any?" I asked handing Ron the frame.

"Every little bit," said Ron smiling. We'll just leave our friend and his evidence where he can be easily found."

"I'll give you all away," said Foulton. "I'll give away your secret."

"What, that a child actor and a famous baseball player are secret agents?" I said. "Oh, and I almost forgot."

I pulled the Loop from my pocket and scrolled to the first picture I had taken of Foulton. I put the Loop near Foulton's face.

"You look good in pictures," I told the evil doctor. "Have you ever considered doing any movies?"

Foulton looked at his photo in disgust. There he was on the screen holding both the painting and the money. He turned away.

"Don't worry, doc," I said. "I'll print you a copy for your jail cell."

Ron reached into a compartment in the helicopter and pulled out some rope.

"Who would like to do the honors?" he said.

I grabbed the rope and set to work tying up Dr. Foulton. It felt good to catch a bad guy.

And we lifted off in pursuit of the rest of the story. I had a feeling that this mission was far from over.

Act 16:
PUZZLE PIECES

After dropping Foulton and the evidence in front of police headquarters, we all went home. The next morning was Saturday. I got up early and ran all the way to Glen's loft. When I arrived, Glen was standing on the ladder, just like we left him, building his Spam tin pyramid higher and higher. His hat was still planted firmly on his head.

"Glen," I said. "Have you finished the script?"

"Oh yes, Marc," he replied. "But this pyramid... that's another story."

I reached into my backpack and pulled out my half of the secret portrait minus the frame.

"Goodness me," said Glen when he saw it. "We're going to need Millenia's help on this one."

Glen climbed down, removed the POKEY from its hiding place under his cap, and turned it on.

CLAP! CLAP! Glen banged his hands together. The lights went out and Millenia's silhouette appeared on the wall.

"Do we have the painting?" was the first question that the mysterious figure asked.

"Sort of," I said showing the silhouette the torn shred of canvas before explaining everything that had happened the night before. Then I pulled out the Loop to show him what the painting had really looked like.

"You may have enough there in your hand," said Millenia.

"Enough," I said. "Enough of what? What's going on here? What is this?"

Millenia breathed deeply and let out a sigh.

"I believe that it's time to tell you all," he said. "There is no other way now. Glen, do you have any tape?"

"Sure," said Glen. He disappeared into the darkness and a moment later reappeared with two pieces of tape.

"Is this enough?" Glen asked.

"Perfect," answered Millenia. "Marc, I need you to do something for me."

"What?"

"Take the painting and tape it up on the wall in front of the POKEY," said Millenia.

I headed over to the wall and placed two pieces of tape on the upper right and left hand corners of the canvas. Then I pressed it to the wall.

"The painting that concealed the secret portrait is not important," began Millenia. "But this is."

Suddenly Millenia's silhouette disappeared. A dim, off-colored light appeared from the POKEY casting its beam on the torn artwork. The remnant glowed revealing something amazing.

The lips and nose of the man in the portrait disappeared! They were replaced with the outline of what appeared to be mountain ranges. The chin formed a coastline and along the creases that bordered the man's jaw showed roads. It was not really a secret portrait but a map.

"What is that?" asked Jim. "What are you shining on the painting?"

"It's a special light," said Millenia's voice from the POKEY. "The map was drawn using a special paint. When the beam is shown on the portrait it makes the special paint underneath glow."

"What does the map lead to?" I asked.

"It leads to me," replied Millenia. "It leads to the place where I hide."

"What!?" we all exclaimed.

"This is the only copy," continued Millenia. "And until now I was the only one who knew of its existence."

"But why didn't you tell any of us?" asked Glen. "Why couldn't the rest of us know?"

"Because this is the greatest of our secrets," answered Millenia. "I used to have one person amongst the order keep the map safe. That person was the guardian and in case I was threatened or in need, that person knew where to find me. It has been that way for as long as I can remember. But when the last guardian gave up his task and went away, I did not choose another."

"Why?" I asked.

"Because Foulton was that last guardian," said Millenia. "Don't forget, he was also once a member of the Order of the Cat. But I did not know that Foulton would come back to claim the map. It has remained hidden in the museum for many years. In fact, I'd nearly forgotten about it."

"You didn't trust us?" I said. "But we trust you, Millenia."

"I'm sorry, Marc," said Millenia. " It's just that I didn't want to risk another one of us going bad. When it happened to Foulton, one of my best students, I thought that it could happen to anyone. Please forgive me."

"But now the Order of the Snake has part of the map," I exclaimed. "Aren't you in danger?"

"Some," replied Millenia. "But you, Marc John Jefferies, have lessened that danger. The half that you were able to wrest away from Trufo is the most important, for it shows exactly where I keep my lair."

"But what about the other half?" asked Glen examining the map on the wall. "When the Order of the Snake gets close enough, it will only be a matter of time before they find you."

"I've already thought of that," said Millenia calmly. "Glen, have you finished that script yet – the one for Marc's new movie?"

"Yes," said Glen. "Finally."

"I'm sorry to hear that," said Millenia. "Because you're going to need to rewrite some of it."

Glen's eyes widened.

"But why!?" he exclaimed.

"Because I'm going to need some help," replied Millenia. "And Marc's going to need a reason to come to southern Italy."

"Southern Italy," I said running over to the map.

"That's right," said Millenia. "For that is where I hide. The world needs you, Marc John Jefferies. Pack your bags. The true adventure is about to begin."

Glen ran to his desk and furiously began dialing numbers into his phone.

"Who are you calling?" I asked.

"Your father," said Glen with a worried look on his face.

Glen waited a moment on the line before speaking...

"Hello, Mr. Jefferies," he said. "Glen Spade here... no sir," he continued. "The movie's not quite done. In fact, there's been a little change in plans..."

...to be continued in BOOK 3: The Volcano.

Marc John Jefferies' Director's Sheet

A.
Abyss - A bottomless pit or hole. It is typically very dark.

Artifacts - Objects made by man and discovered by later generations.

C.
Chandelier - An elaborate and ornate light fixture that hangs from the ceiling.

Corridors - Long hallways.

D.
Decipher - To break or understand a code.

F.
Fluorescent Lights - The long and very bright (almost glowing) light bulbs that are in school classrooms. Fluorescent light bulbs are much brighter than regular light bulbs but they use six times less energy.

Furrowed - With deep and narrow grooves or cracks (like big wrinkles across the forehead).

G.

Gawk - To look unblinking at something in amazement or wonder.

Global Positioning System (GPS) - An electronic device that allows users to determine exactly where they are. The GPS "talks" to the satellites placed in orbit around our planet. The satellite technology was developed by the United States Military and has been modified for use in cars and cell phones.

H.

Horizon - The line in the distance where it appears that the ground and the sky meet and blend together.

M.

Morsel - A tiny scrap or leftover food.

Mummy - The body of a person prepared for burial, wrapped and decorated according with ancient Egyptian tradition.

N.

Navigated - Directed the course of a car, a boat or an airplane. Did you know that large boats like cruise ships and cargo ships, as well as airplanes, have people that serve just as navigators? Their job is to sit next to the pilot or captain and give them directions.

P.

Perplexed - Bewildered, puzzled, or very confused.

Prism - A solid glass object with many facets, used to direct and scatter light beams.

R.

Radiant - Glowing with light.

S.

Sarcophagus - A very decorative stone box or coffin used by the ancient Egyptians to bury a mummy.

Silhouette - A dark shadow or outline seen against a light background.

V.

Valet - A male servant. In today's world, the most common valets are the people that park cars outside of restaurants and hotels.

Marc John Jefferies' Gyroscope

American Revolution - The American Revolution is also known as the War for Independence. American colonists fought the British to become an independent country. The Declaration of Independence and the Constitution we have today came out of the American Revolution against the British.

British - Citizens of Great Britain, a country across the Atlantic Ocean from the United States, in Europe. England is part of Great Britain and the ruling government for all the other territories. Great Britain is a much older country than the United States. It is from the British settlers that we get the English language we now speak in America and parts of Canada. After the American Revolution ended, the British/English people have become good friends of the United States.

Declaration of Independence - The document adopted by the Congress of the United States on July 4, 1776 that established the United States as an independent country. You can still view the original Declaration of Independence. It is on display at the National Archives in Washington , D.C.

Egypt - A magnificent country in North Africa and part of the Middle East. It was known in the ancient world for its advanced culture and beautiful architecture. Egypt was the home of two of the seven wonders of the ancient world: the pyramids, and the Great Library at Alexandria. It was here that many of the world's most intelligent people came to study and learn. Did you know that Egypt is seven times the size of the State of New Mexico?

George Washington - George Washington was a General in the American Revolutionary War and was elected as the first President of the United States. He was known for his bravery and dedication to the new American People.
It is interesting to note that George Washington did not live in the White House and that his home was not in Washington, D.C. The Capital of the United States actually was moved from Virginia to Annapolis and then to New York, before it eventually came to Washington, D.C.

Patriots - People with a deep love for their country, like the American colonists who were dedicated to defend the freedom and insure America's independence from Great Britain.

www.marcjohnonline.com

Fighting alongside his quirky sidekick, Scooter Brosnan, Marc embarks on a series of adventures that carry him to multiple countries to face multiple foes. On the trail, he finds his way into and out of trouble, greets mystery and intrigue with a joke and a smile, and even bumps into a little romance - all while acting for the camera and finishing his homework!

The Secret Agent MJJ series is a thrill ride through life's lessons and adventures and has a universal appeal that is sure to delight boys and girls of all ages. Discover and learn with Marc John Jefferies in a way that only MJJ, The Real Deal, can provide.

Need more adventure and excitement?
Visit
www.marcjohnonline.com

to find information on a Marc John Jefferies Adventure Party coming to a city near you. And be sure to look for these spectacular new titles on the website or the shelves of your local bookstore.

#1: The Missing Princess
#2: The Secret Portrait

...and next:

#3: The Volcano
Marc meets up with new friends and companions as they travel into the center of a rumbling volcano. Will they keep the mountain from erupting or will The Order of the Snake prevail in its quest for world domination and chaos? Follow Marc as he throws himself into harms way to stop a disaster that is anything but natural.

Wait! There's more!

Coming soon...

#4: The Fountain of Youth
#5: The Pirates of Marathon
#6: The Sun King
#7: The Mad Conductor

Go see Marc's movies!

www.marcjohnonline.com

Marc on the small screen...

This is Roy, the character Marc John Jefferies plays on Mr. Bill Cosby's new animated show, "Fatherhood." See it on Nickelodeon.

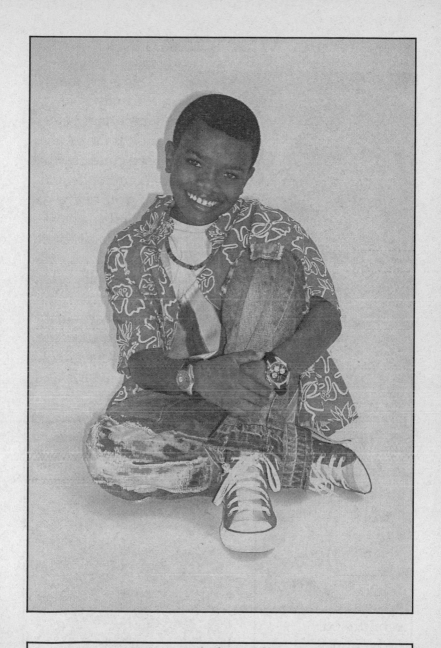

www.marcjohnonline.com

Meet Marc's family ....

This is my family. Family is very important to me. It is the ideal structure of your community and well being. Family is what living is all about. As Secret Agent MJJ, I will protect this world from any harm that would effect the precious gift of family.

Look forward to my little brother's series:
"Nano's World."

- Ages 1-5 years old
- picture stories
- childhood adventures